IN THE GHOST DETECTIVE UNIVERSE:

NOVELS
(Best to be read in order)
Beyond the Grave
Unveiling the Past
Beneath the Surface

SHORT STORIES
(All stand-alone)
Just Desserts
Lost Friends
Family Bonds
Common Ground
Till Death
Family History
Heritage
Eternal Bond
New Beginnings
Severed Ties

Lost Friends
by R.W. Wallace

Copyright © 2021 by R.W. Wallace

Copy editing by Jinxie Gervasio
Cover by the author
Cover Illustration 10926765 © germanjames | 123rf.com
Cover Illustration 58372685 © perseomedusa | 123rf.com
Cover Illustration 263199440 © Nouman | Adobe Stock

All characters and events in this book, other than those clearly in the public domain, are fictitious and any resemblance to real persons, living or dead, is purely coincidental.

All rights reserved. No part of this publication may be reproduced, distributed, or transmitted in any form or by any means, including photocopying, recording, or other electronic or mechanical methods, without the prior written permission of the publisher, except in the case of brief quotations embodied in critical reviews and certain other noncommercial uses permitted by copyright law. For permission requests, write to the publisher, addressed "Attention: Permissions Coordinator," at the address below.

www.rwwallace.com

ISBN: [979-10-95707-15-8]

Main category—Fiction
Other category—Mystery

First Edition

R.W. WALLACE

AUTHOR OF THE TOLOSA MYSTERY SERIES

LOST FRIENDS

A Ghost Detective Short Story

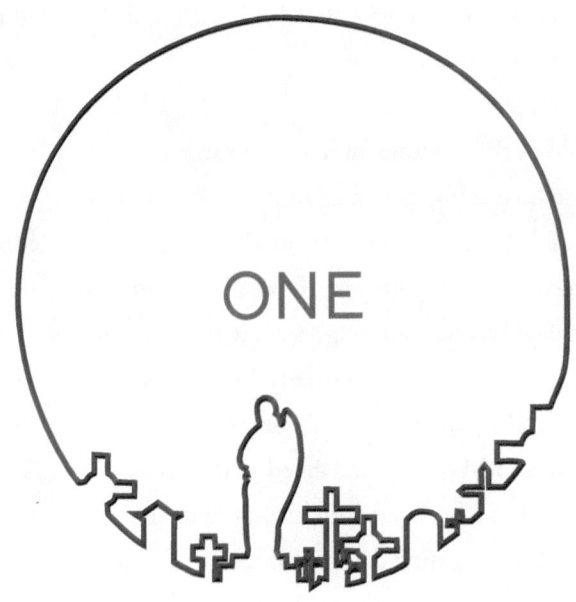

ONE

At the farthest corner of the cemetery, a very special mausoleum stands vigil. It's not particularly pretty, nor gaudy, nor pious. It's tall, solid, and spacious.

Some call it the pauper's grave, but that's not quite right, either.

From what I've understood, the mausoleum was paid for according to the last wishes of a retired police detective, to give a final resting place to the Jane and John Does of the district, the bodies nobody claimed, nobody wanted.

The detective's urn is in there as well, in the spot directly across from the entrance, watching over all his charges.

At least, I imagine that was the idea. Except, as far as I know, the detective didn't linger after his burial, and the guarding has been left to us other ghosts.

Not that I mind.

Today, the mausoleum has a new arrival.

I stand leaning against Clothilde's tombstone as we watch the party of three make their way from the church. Two police officers and one priest. The youngest of the officers carries a simple, white urn against his chest, his fingers white from clutching it too hard.

He can't be more than twenty-five, probably fresh out of the academy. His hair is dark and curly despite being cut short, his eyes large and brown—and filled with unshed tears. While his colleague has a whispered discussion with the priest, the young man is clearly fighting demons in his own head as he focuses on their destination.

"Doesn't seem like we're getting a new friend," Clothilde comments. She's pretending to sit on her tombstone. I say pretend because she's sitting at the right height, just not in the right location. Not wanting to get too close to me, she sits mid-air right next to the slab of black stone, hands beneath her thighs and swinging her legs.

Most of us try to respect the physical laws of the living even if we don't have to. Clothilde doesn't.

"Doesn't hurt to stay to watch," I reply. "A couple of extra witnesses."

When the small procession passes us, we stand to follow. I sidle up right behind the older officer and the priest, unapologetically eavesdropping.

"How old did you say she was?" the priest asks in a whisper.

"Nine or ten. Probably. Hard to tell when they're undernourished like that."

"You're certain she was murdered, didn't just die of hunger?"

The officer's torso swells as it fills with anger. "I'd argue that a kid dying of hunger *is* a murder." He deflates a little. "But yeah. Marks on her neck, skin under her nails, bruises all over. She was murdered."

"So you have DNA?"

"No match." A sigh. "If he ever pops up in our database later, we'll nail him, but right now we're stuck."

I share a look with Clothilde. Sounds like someone who'd have unfinished business, who'd want to stick around for a bit to tie up loose ends. But the silence from the urn says otherwise.

A coffin or urn will only let a ghost free once he or she has accepted they're dead. This usually means days of screaming and pounding.

A silent urn means the girl has already moved on.

"You have nothing?" the priest asks. His eyes glide over to the younger officer walking in front of him, compassion marking his features.

The older officer huffs. "Normally, I'd tell you I can't talk about an ongoing investigation, but there's really nothing to tell. All we have is a dead body and useless DNA."

"Where was she found?"

"At the bottom of a cliff in the forest outside of town. She was dead before she was thrown down there," he adds before the priest can ask. "It seems they considered that ravine like a convenient place to throw away a body." His voice lowers. "Was found by a couple of young boys going on an adventure."

We reach the mausoleum and the priest takes the urn. He slides it into the designated slot and closes the little door.

Like with most of the slots here, there is no name, only a cross and a date of death.

The priest says a few words, more than he usually does in here—I'm guessing it's for the young officer's benefit, who seems on the verge of collapsing from keeping his tears back—then they turn to leave.

Clothilde and I stay back, on the front steps of the mausoleum, and watch them exit the cemetery. The priest goes back to the church, the two officers leave in an unmarked car.

"Who are you?" says a voice from behind us. "Where am I?"

I whirl around. If I'd had a beating heart, it might just have stopped beating.

In the middle of the mausoleum, dirty feet on the black-and-white checkered floor, stands a girl of nine or ten. Malnourished and so thin it's painful to watch, large clear eyes staring at me.

"Where are my friends?" she asks. "They were supposed to be here."

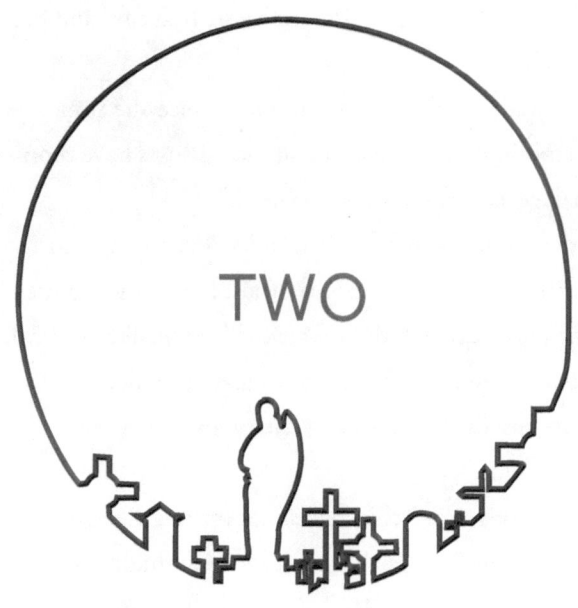

TWO

"Where are my friends?" the girl asks again when she gets no answer from us, her voice serious. Her arms hang limply at her side, almost swallowed in the several-sizes-too-big t-shirt she's wearing.

I finally find my voice. "I'm afraid your friends aren't here, honey."

She flashes her teeth in a snarl and hisses. "Don't call me honey."

I raise my hands in surrender. "Okay, I won't. I promise. Do you have a name, perhaps?"

Her distrust is clear as she considers whether or not to give me her name. Her gaze takes in the mausoleum, the cemetery outside, the gray-scale ghosts talking to her. "Rose," she says.

"That's a lovely name," I tell her. "It suits you."

"No, it doesn't," she spits. "Roses are beautiful and full of life. Roses are free."

Clothilde speaks in that midnight voice she sometimes uses when emotions are close to the surface. "Roses have thorns. They can make even the biggest man bleed."

Rose studies Clothilde. I wonder if she knows to recognize clothes that were at the height of fashion in the eighties. If she sees the anger that Clothilde carries like a blanket but will never share with anyone. If she sees the danger lurking.

Rose smiles. "I like you. What's your name?"

"Clothilde."

Rose nods, a mischievous smile making her go from street urchin to long-lost warrior princess. "Clothilde, you and I are going to be the best of friends."

Somehow, I don't think that means what I think it means.

Clothilde knows it, too. She takes her time considering the little girl in front of us, measuring her up against God knows what. She gives a tiny nod. "Done."

"Excellent." Rose claps her hands as if to get the party going. "Now, where are my friends?"

I've never had to do this before. Something must have gone wrong with the urn, because it's not supposed to let her out until she knows she's a ghost. This girl just walked out thinking she must have fallen asleep or something, and expects to find her friends.

I have to tell her she's dead.

"Your friends aren't here, Rose," I explain. "Something

happened to you, and now you're…" I wave a hand to the cemetery behind me. "You're dead."

I hold my breath, waiting for the denial or the panic. Or both.

Rose rolls her eyes at me. "I know I'm dead, stupid. You don't think I'd remember dying?"

I'm floored, unable to catch a breath I don't need, my brain not able to wrap itself around what she said.

"You know you're dead?" I ask. Maybe I heard her wrong.

Rose's eyes wander from my head to my toes, then comes back up. "You don't?"

I blink. Shake myself back into action. "Of course I know I'm dead. I've been here for over thirty years." I fall down on my knees so I'm not towering above the little girl. "How did *you* know?"

She shrugs and flashes an uncertain look at Clothilde. "It's what always happens when one of us is brought into the woods in the middle of the night. It was either me or Violette," she explains when she doesn't understand why I look so shocked. "We're the oldest."

"How many of you are there?" I whisper.

"Twelve," Rose answers. "But I think he has his eyes on a new one, so he had to make room for her."

"A new what?" I think I know the answer, but I have to ask.

"A new girl. He likes 'em young and smooth," she says. She's mimicking a coarse accent, what you'd expect from a guy living in the middle of nowhere. "Puberty is messy," she continues. "Doesn't want to deal with that."

Puberty? "How old are you?"

For the first time, she looks uncertain. She stares down at her bare feet. "I don't know. I was five when he got me."

"And how did he 'get you?'"

"Snatched me in the park. Drove for a long time. Put me in the house."

I sit back on my heels, mind reeling.

Clothilde takes over the questioning. "Why did you expect to meet your friends here, if you know you're a ghost?"

Rose wraps her arms around herself, as if she can feel the cold. "Everybody comes back when they're taken to the woods. They keep us company. Look after us."

Clothilde swears under her breath. "They come back as ghosts when they die?"

Rose nods.

"And you could see them?"

Rose pulls a face. "Not really see them. Feel them. They'll sit with us when we're punished, keep us company when it's our turn with the old man. Sing to us when we can't sleep."

"Old man?"

"It's what he wanted us to call him."

Clothilde paces back and forth inside the mausoleum, her feet a couple of inches above the floor. "If they stay in the house as ghosts," she says to me, "it means they're buried nearby."

"Probably," I say. I'm still on my knees in front of the little girl. I want to give her a hug, but don't think it's a good idea. "We don't have experience with anyone buried outside of the cemetery. We don't know how it works out there."

Clothilde points her thumb at Rose. "Why didn't he bury her with the rest of them?"

I shake my head as I ponder this new mystery.

"Did the old man ever get bothered by the ghosts?" I ask.

Rose nods. "When there are many ghosts together, we can feel them better. Some time ago, Petunia came back earlier than usual because the old man started freaking out. She said our friends helped her."

Clothilde stopped her pacing and cocked her head at Rose. "Why do you all have flower names?"

"It's the names he gives us when we arrive. If you try to tell anyone your real name, you get taken into the woods straight away."

Clothilde puts a hand on the girl's shoulder, her voice soft. "What's your real name, sweetheart?"

Rose flinches at the nickname but doesn't say anything. I'm guessing we should stay away from any nickname that bastard of an old man could have used.

"You can tell us," I say. "He can't hurt you now, you're already dead."

She chews on her lip and her breathing accelerates. "Lena," she finally whispers.

"That suits you even better than Rose," Clothilde says with a smile. "I'm very happy to be your friend, Lena."

Lena smiles, but it's wobbly. Her eyes fill with tears and she hugs her arms closer around herself. "I want my friends."

I force myself not to take the girl in my arms. I'm afraid she won't appreciate being held by a man right now.

Luckily, Clothilde has the same impulse and envelops the girl in her arms, making the thin body almost disappear in her adult one. "We'll help you, Lena." She pulls the little girl's head away from her breast so she can look her in the eye. "But I don't think that what you really need is to meet your friends."

Tears streak down Lena's cheeks as she starts to whine.

"What you need," Clothilde says forcefully enough to get through to the little girl, "is to make sure the old man is punished. And save your living friends."

As the words register, the whines subside. Hiccups start up and the tears keep falling, but Lena's eyes widen in wonder. "I can do that?"

"There are no guarantees," I say as I push myself into a standing position. There are days like this, where I feel the age of my body despite not having felt my body in over three decades. "But we'll do our best to help you."

THREE

"We're going to need outside help," I tell Clothilde. We're sitting on the steps of Lena's mausoleum while the girl makes the tour of the cemetery. We told her she wouldn't be able to leave, but—like all of us—she has to see it for herself.

"We *always* need outside help," Clothilde replies. "It's just a question of giving a nudge to the right person. In this case, there's a good chance we won't have any visitors—unless that sniveling officer comes back."

I tap my fingers on my thigh. "You know, there's a good chance he will. If he was that torn up about the case, he's not going to let it go."

"You did." Her voice is soft and her eyes distant.

"Which is why I'm here, still." I sigh. "And I didn't bawl my eyes out like that guy—he'll be back. We have to figure out what to do when he does."

"What do we want from him, exactly?"

"We need to give him clues," I say. "They said they were without leads, but we have information we can give them. Like a name."

"Is that all?" Clothilde rolls her eyes and leans back on her hands. "You know as well as I do that we can give them nudges or communicate really strong feelings. We can't spell out a name for them."

She's right, of course. The height of influence we have on the living world is swatting away a fly or blowing dust across the floor...

"We *can* spell it out!" I jump up and run over to the little door that's hiding Lena's urn. In front of the door, there's a small ledge. Spotless, because everything was cleaned before a new urn arrived, but it doesn't need to stay that way.

"Clothilde." I wave her over. "You're much better at this than me. Can you blow in some dust from the path outside, do you think? Get some of it up here? Then we should be able to spell the name in the dust."

I can see that Clothilde's first reaction is to refuse. A part of her is stuck as the rebellious teenager, but it only comes out occasionally. Now she glances over to the cemetery's back gate, where Lena has climbed the gate and is giving it her all to fall down on the other side.

"I'll give it a try," she says. "But there's no way I'll manage to cover only that ledge," she warns me. "This whole place is going to be a mess."

I stretch my arms out, leaving her the floor. "Have at it."

☙

She wasn't kidding about the mess. By the time she's done, there's a thick layer of dust all across the floor. The ledge in front of the urn's door has such a thin layer it's barely visible.

"That ledge is really high up," Clothilde says as she levels the ledge with a murderous stare.

"No worries," I tell her. "You did a great job. This should do the trick."

I step up to the ledge and hold a finger above the dust. I focus everything I have on making my finger as solid as possible, and on the fine particles I'd like to behave as if I had a solid form.

I don't get it on the first try, nor the tenth, of course. But I persevere. If there's something we have an infinite supply of here, it's time. So I stay in front of that ledge, pushing my finger through the dust over and over, until lines appear.

It's well into the next day when I declare myself finished. Clothilde has come and gone, spending the most time with Lena. The girl didn't have trouble accepting she was a ghost, but she's unable to grasp being stuck here, and not with her dead friends in the forest.

Two days later, the young officer is back. This time, he's alone and he's not trying to put on a brave face.

He shuffles into the mausoleum, head down and a single tear running down his chin.

When he sees all the dust on the floor, he freezes. "What the—"

He spins around in a circle, taking in the mess Clothilde made. His mouth is hanging open, his eyes are bugging out, his breathing is shallow.

"Who would do this?" He stomps around in a circle, kicking up dust, repeating with increasing volume, "Who would do this?"

"Go check on the urn, buddy," I tell him.

People can't actually hear us, of course. But their subconscious must hear us on some level, because most people will take a nudge.

The officer takes his time about it, though. In fact, he makes such a mess of—well, our mess—that I worry he'll ruin my work. I keep telling him to approach the ledge, check on the urn. And *finally*, he calms down and does as I tell him.

He stalks up to the little door. "I'm going to find out who did this," he fumes. "I'm going to find out who killed you, and who did this to your grave. I—"

He cuts himself short as he sees the writing. "What—?"

His head snaps around so fast, I cringe in compassion. He takes in the mess, and I see the moment he realizes he might have ruined potential evidence. He didn't, of course, but there's no way for me to tell him that.

"It was all smooth when I came in," he says to himself. "There were no footsteps. I would have noticed if there were footsteps." He puts his nose an inch above the writing on the ledge. "Then how did they write this? Lena?"

He straightens, and his eyes go to the door hiding the urn. "Was that your name, little one?"

"Yes, it was." Lena herself has come, Clothilde at her heels. "My name was Lena."

The officer nods. "Guess it's worth looking into."

He snaps a few pictures but leaves only a minute or two later. He has a spring to his step that I'm happy to see.

Lena slinks back out, Clothilde in tow, to try every single spot along the cemetery wall, in search of her friends.

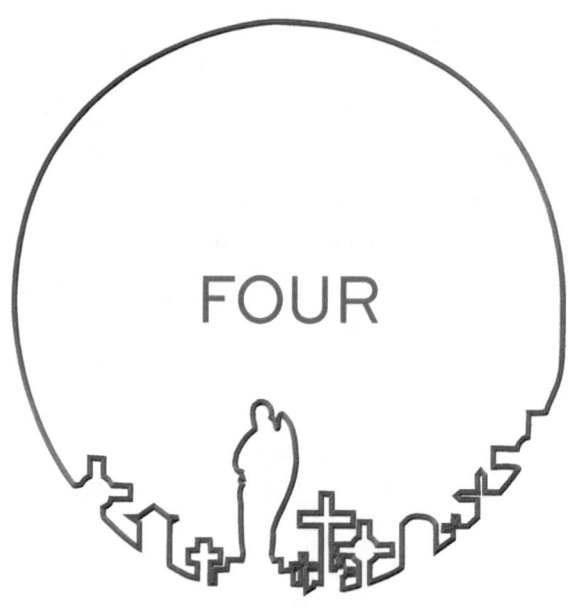

FOUR

It's at least ten days until we get new visitors to the mausoleum. Lena has accepted that she can't leave the cemetery grounds, but she's no less restless.

On a bright Sunday morning, a couple in their late thirties park their car in the church's parking lot and walk slowly through the cemetery. A police car arrived with them, but the driver—our young officer from earlier if I'm not mistaken—doesn't get out.

The woman's none too steady on her feet and I suspect the man's only doing better because he has the task of taking care of his wife.

I wait for them at the mausoleum. Lena and Clothilde join me, silent and serious.

"Do you remember these people?" I ask Lena.

A frown mars her little forehead and her hands are balled into fists at her sides. "I don't… I can't… I… Mommy?"

She steps forward, just in time for her mother to step right through her.

"Sorry about that," Clothilde says before the girl can get too upset. "Follow them inside. See what they have to say."

We all follow. Lena stands right in front of her resting place the better to see her parents' faces, while Clothilde and myself keep a respectful distance.

"I can't believe you were alive all these years," the mother sobs. "I'm so sorry we weren't able to find you, darling." She places a hand on the little door, not realizing she's touching her daughter's ghost face.

Lena has the expression of an innocent five-year-old, not the weathered and angry ten-or-so-old we've gotten used to. The love in her eyes as she looks at her mother is blinding.

"At least now you can rest," the mother whispers. "I can't believe that's the best we can do."

"It's not all we can do," the father says. His voice is no steadier than his wife's and his worry lines are too deep for someone his age. "We'll also help the police find whoever did this to her."

The anger comes back to Lena's features. "The old man," she tells them. "He was mean to us. Hurt me. Hurt my friends. I miss my friends, Mommy. They need me."

The mother shakes her head, as if to remove cobwebs.

"I think she hears you," I say. "Continue talking about the old man. Try remembering what it was like there, and in the forest. Anything to help them find your friends."

She does as I tell her. What follows is a harrowing account of all the horrors she saw in that house in the woods, and of her friends, alive kids and ghosts alike.

The mother breaks down into sobs, only her husband holding her up. She won't understand why she feels this way, but I'm guessing she's gotten the gist of her daughter's message.

"See the writing in the dust, like the officer mentioned?" the husband says once she starts to calm down. "Somebody knew who she was and wanted her to be reconnected with her family."

Wiping away tears, the mother stares at my masterpiece. "This was done by a friend," she says. "Whoever did this to her didn't want her to be identified." She lifts her gaze to meet her husband's, the same determination we've seen in Lena as she attempted escape shining through. "We have to find that friend."

"The forest." Clothilde has moved closer, so close her mouth is superposed with the woman's ear. "Try the forest. Where she was found."

"The forest." Lena adds her voice in. "Search the forest, Mommy. Help my friends."

The mother sways on her feet, leans a hand against the wall. "Wasn't she found in a forest? How well did they search that place?"

"I think they did a pretty thorough search," the husband replies.

"Well, they're going to be more thorough. That officer told us they suspect whoever did this was behind at least ten other kidnappings in our town. If they're looking for ten kids instead of just one, they can damned well search ten times as far. They have to go through that whole thing!"

The husband kisses his wife's temple. "It's a pretty big forest, honey."

"They're going to search that forest. Or I'll never let them rest."

The husband nods. "Then that's what they'll do."

"Thank you, Mommy," Lena whispers. She leans in to give her mother a hug—she even gets it right the first time and doesn't go straight through.

Once her parents have driven away, Lena joins me on the steps of her mausoleum. "Do you think they'll find them?"

"It's out of our hands now, little one," I tell her. "But I hope they do. I really hope they do."

FIVE

They did find the house. The old man—I still don't know his real name, and don't care to know—had had enough of the ghosts haunting his house and decided to get rid of the bodies farther away from his house. He'd walked far enough with Lena's body for the search party not to have reached his home on their first trip through, but not far enough to resist the search party Lena's mother managed to set up with the parents of the ten other missing children.

The old man was arrested and is expected to spend the rest of his life in jail.

The twelve girls—one who'd arrived just two days after Lena's death as her replacement, also named Rose—who still lived at the house, were sent straight to the hospital for a check-up, then reunited with their families.

The parents who hadn't found their children requested a detailed check of the grounds around the house.

We learned all of this from Lena's mother, who came to give us daily updates. She'd clearly caught onto the importance her daughter put in saving her friends and made sure she knew they were now safe at home with their families. They'd have some tough times ahead, but they'd live.

She'd also promised a surprise for today, which had all of us, including Clothilde who never got excited about anything, checking the parking lot every two minutes, asking each other what we thought the surprise would be.

Finally, as the sun approaches the horizon, a van pulls into the parking lot, and Lena's parents exit. As they start pulling open the back doors, several other cars follow, each one containing a couple or a family.

Every couple goes to the van, gets something from the back, and walks solemnly toward the cemetery.

"They're urns," Lena whispers.

I nod.

As the first couple passes the gate to the cemetery, a ghost exits the urn and looks around. It's a girl.

"Iris!" Lena exclaims and runs to throw herself at the new arrival. "They brought Iris! And Lily!"

A second girl has jumped out of the next urn, held by a Chinese couple accompanied by a boy of about five.

They're all here. Ghost tears run freely as the girls are reunited, touching each other's faces, giving kisses, screaming so loud I'm glad I no longer have ear drums.

The families all make their way to the mausoleum. They wait outside, letting Lena's mother go in first.

"Come, Lena," I tell her. "Let's see what your mother has to say."

We all squeeze in, the girls hovering above us in the air, clearly used to not respecting physical laws.

"I brought your friends, honey," Lena's mother says to her daughter's slot. "We found the place that awful man used as a mass grave. Now, we could all have brought you home to our cemeteries, but we didn't want to separate you."

A couple of mothers nod their heads at this, making me realize Lena must not be the only one to have influenced her parents.

"So we've brought you all here. The police told us it was okay, that it was the least they could do to repay us for finding the man who murdered you.

"Now you can play together as much as you like." A tear falls down her face and lands on the dirty floor with a plop.

What follows is a procession of families deposing the urns of their daughters' ashes in the mausoleum. There's not a dry eye in sight, living or ghosts alike.

When the families finally leave, I'm left with a host of young girls.

Who are already becoming more transparent.

Lena looks down at herself, then asks, "Is this it? Do we not get to play?"

If there was ever a group of kids who deserved to play, it was this one.

"I'm sure you'll be allowed to play where you're going," I tell her. "Take a good hold of each other's hands and stay together, okay?"

I have no idea if there's any point in doing it, but the girls follow my instructions. They all fade out at the same time just as a peal of joyous laughter sounds across the cemetery.

Clothilde stares longingly at the spot where Lena stood moments earlier. "You did good, detective." Then she ambles across the grounds toward her own tombstone.

I swallow and think back on all my cases, before and after my death. This goes a good way toward redemption, I think, but there's still a long way to go.

A long, long way.

AUTHOR'S NOTE

THANK YOU FOR reading *Lost Friends*. I hope you enjoyed it!

This story is part of a series. I'm having a blast writing the stories and am not ready to let Robert and Clothilde go straight away, so you can expect more of these stories to pop up. They all appear first in *Pulphouse Fiction Magazine* before I publish them individually.

There's also a series of novels in the same universe, with the same characters (where they get to investigate their own murders!) so make sure to look out for those. The first book is called *Beyond the Grave*.

If you liked the story, you might want to check out some of my other books mentioned on the next page. It's mostly Mysteries, but a few Science Fiction short stories will pop up, too.

R.W. Wallace
www.rwwallace.com

ABOUT THE AUTHOR

R.W. WALLACE WRITES in most genres, though she tends to end up in mystery more often than not. Dead bodies keep popping up all over the place whenever she sits down in front of her keyboard.

The stories mostly take place in Norway or France; the country she was born in and the one that has been her home for two decades. Don't ask her why she writes in English—she won't have a sensible answer for you.

Her Ghost Detective short story series appears in *Pulphouse Magazine*, starting in issue #9.

You can find all her books, long and short, all genres, on rwwallace.com.

Also by R.W. Wallace

Mystery

Ghost Detective Novels
Beyond the Grave
Unveiling the Past
Beneath the Surface

Ghost Detective Shorts
Just Desserts
Lost Friends
Family Bonds
Common Ground
Till Death
Family History
Heritage
Eternal Bond
New Beginnings
Severed Ties

The Tolosa Mystery Series
The Red Brick Haze
The Red Brick Cellars
The Red Brick Basilica

Short Story Collections
Deep Dark Secrets
A Thief in the Night

Short Stories
Cold Blue Eternity
Hidden Horrors

Critters
Gertrude and the Trojan Horse
First Impressions
Let Them Eat Cake
Out of Sight
Sitting Duck
Two's Company
Like Mother Like Daughter

Romance

French Office Romance Series
Flirting in Plain Sight
Hiding in Plain Sight
Loving in Plain Sight

Fantasy (short stories)
Unexpected Consequences
Morbier Impossible
A Second Chance

Science Fiction (short stories)
The Vanguard

Lollapalooza Shorts
Quarantine
Common Enemies
Coiled Danger
Mars Meeting

Adventure (short stories)
Size Matters

www.ingramcontent.com/pod-product-compliance
Lightning Source LLC
LaVergne TN
LVHW041717060526
838201LV00043B/784